AF377982

A STRANGE KIND OF PARADISE

A LIFE WORTH LIVING

A

NOVELLA

HETTIE ASHWIN

Published by Slipperygrip 2021

A strange kind of paradise.
Novella: A life worth living
Copyright Hettie Ashwin

All rights reserved

The moral right of the author has been asserted.
This book is sold subject to the condition that it shall not, by way of trade or otherwise, be lent, re-sold, hired out, or otherwise circulated without the author's proper consent in any form other than that in which it is published and without a similar condition including this condition being imposed on the subsequent purchaser.

ISBN: **9782491490195**
POCKET EDITION
ISBN: 9782491490201

www.hettieashwin.blogspot.com
facebook.com/alacrity.vivacity

Books by Hettie Ashwin

<u>Humour</u>
Literary Licence
The Reluctant Messiah
Mr Tripp buys a lifestyle
Barney's Test
The Truffle War
Fat Bits
Murder! Mayhem! and lesser cuts of meat.
I'd rather glue me nut sack to a bullet train

<u>Memoir</u>
Boat to Baguette
Living it up in France

<u>Thriller</u>
The Crowing of the Beast

<u>Speculative fiction</u>
The Mask of Deceit
Pi - trilogy

<u>Short Stories</u>
After the Rains & other Stories
A shilling on the Bar

<u>Non fiction</u>
Productive Procrastination

<u>Novella series</u>
A strange kind of paradise 1-5

Music expresses that which cannot be put into words and that which cannot remain silent"
— **Victor hugo**

$$\text{\textasciimacron\textasciimacron\textasciimacron\textasciimacron\,\musicalnote\,\textasciimacron\textasciimacron\textasciimacron\textasciimacron}$$

♪

1

'Since when?' I looked at my mother and narrowed my eyes. She sat at my kitchen table and calmly wove a story of enormous proportions on how she has always eaten fish, how she used to fish as a young girl, how she loved fish.

She did not eat fish.

My mother had never eaten fish, and as far as I could recall she hated the stuff. But, dementia does funny things to a person.

She ate the fish.

It wasn't the ideal situation. I had been living as I chose for more years than I cared to remember. Then, as my parents aged they needed help. First it was the cleaner, then the twice a week check by the nurse, then the move to a smaller unit. I helped them pack. A lifetime of stuff had to be culled. Souvenirs of a life lived all jostled for a place in the new home. Things that had been long forgotten reared their head to elicit memories, some good, some bad. I had to be ruthless with my parent's life. Their private life was on display, and it un-nerved them. They were deposited in new surroundings and I left them to process the move.

'More manageable,' the nurse said.

'You have support,' I offered. 'There are plenty of people around the place. You could do things with them.'

'It's a retirement village, where you go to die,' said my father. He missed his shed, his things, his independence and I could understand that. I could put myself in his place and shuddered at the thought of going somewhere for the last time. And it was his last time.

He left my mother, and her world fell apart. They had been together for nearly sixty years and she railed against the injustice, the loneliness.

'It wasn't supposed to be like this. I wanted to go first,' she said. I had no answer.

The grief took every ounce of energy she had left in her little frail body. The amputation of her other half just about killed her, the forgetting to eat nearly finished the job.

'We need a plan.' Her doctor looked at me and raised his eyebrows. Of course we needed a plan. My mother was willing herself

2

to follow my father. She had nothing in her life, nothing to live for. It was a trite, almost glib homily that rang true.

Her life was her husband's life. She was born in a time when the pinnacle of success was to get married and have children. She fulfilled her part of the bargain and then never stretched beyond the homemaker. She read books. She knitted. She cooked tea every night, tucked a hankie in her sleeve, and swept the kitchen floor.

As a child I often wondered what she did all day. I saw other mother's working, golfing, volunteering and driving. My mother did none of this. She disappeared into books and stayed there, as my father went to work and came home for nigh on 55 years. It didn't look like she had ambitions, schemes, dreams, or any vitality for living. She did what she did and that was enough; or so it seemed to me.

I left home as soon as I could, running as fast as I could into adventure, travel, schemes and dreams. I took the high road and the low road. I threw off the staid, porridge of a life my family lived and thrived on the thrill. I'd write home recounting daring adventures, close calls and near misses, hoping I'd bring some of the breathlessness of living into the family home. If I did, it never showed. My parents were 'of an era' that was fast disappearing. They did what they'd always done. My mother ironed her tea towels and carried on, until she didn't.

And so, a plan was devised. I had a spare room. She would come to live with me.

It is an easy thing to say, but harder to put in practice. I would need to think for someone else after years of thinking only for myself.

My mother looked painfully thin. She gathered up her few mementos and placed them on my mantel piece. Now, it would be her mantel piece too.

I suggested a walk around the neighbourhood, to get her bearings. It was then I realised my mother wasn't how I remembered her. Her step was slower, her stance a little stooped and her conversation a bit of an effort. I would need to reconsider the ramifications of living with an elderly person.

There is a fine line between living with someone and coddling them into old age. I went from, put your stuff over there, straight into stirring her tea for her. The funny thing was I enjoyed being the carer and I can only put it down to my latent mothering instincts.

I would cook meals, set out her clothes for the day, tell her where we were going and gradually I began to take over her whole life. It was the easy option to just put her where I wanted. She became an object. She slotted into my routine and was just another item I put on my list, another chore to navigate in my life; something I could project my virtue onto as I buttoned up her shirt and washed her hair. It was control and I had my finger on the button.

My mother slipped into dependency so easily it was unnerving. She let herself be led. And I realised she had been doing it all her life.

When my father died it was a shock, naturally, but the thing that really frightened my mother was the thought of making a decision. She'd never had to make one. My father controlled what they watched on television, when to move the sprinkler, the banking. My mother just did her duty. My father wasn't a bad man, he just wanted things to tick along, and the way to do that, was to do it all himself. My mother went the easy route. She cooked what he liked. She didn't garden, she didn't interfere in the shed, she let her husband do it all. And they lived for sixty years in separate bubbles. I never heard her say,

'I like that music.'

My mother didn't have, or had lost the capacity to think for herself. She didn't eat, not because she was grieving, although the depression might have been the spark, no, she didn't eat because she didn't know what to buy.

She said, 'Your father always bought the meat,' and 'Oh, I just don't know what to get.'

When my father was gone, I got a frantic phone call about the outside tap. My mother didn't know how the thing worked. It had a sprinkler timer on it.

'Well, the garden will just die.' She threw up her hands and that was that. There was no spark of enquiry about how to get it working. Nothing to suggest she might work it out. The garden would die.

Life was too hard and every enquiry was met with, 'oh, your father used to do that.'

As she said the words to me while sitting on her bed in my spare room, I wondered if she realised what those words meant to her, to her life. Would it be cruel to ask, to pry into her feeling at this stage of her life? Would it bring up the longing, the hopes dashed, the dreams shredded into little pieces for the sake of home and hearth?

We had never had a strong relationship. I looked at my mother dispassionately. Here was a woman who was a blank canvas. Did she have any memories to fall back on? Could she recount a particular time in her life when it was filled with joy?

As I smoothed the quilt and looked around her room I wondered if she felt a failure. Not that success is measured by a yardstick of experiences, education, achievements. Success doesn't really rely on a benchmark, but rather a feeling that it turned out alright in the end. If I asked my mother, I mused on how she might process the question. It might just destroy her, or what little of her there was left after her years of marriage. Was the woman still in there, or had she been replaced by something that was foreign to me? I guess the question I really wanted to ask was,

'Who are you?'

$$\underline{\quad\quad\quad}\ \text{\musicalnote}\ \underline{\quad\quad}$$

2

It is hard to make your home someone else's home too. I had an eclectic mix of furniture, things that I'd collected as I moved, travelled and lived life. I prided myself on squeezing every last drop of the elixir of living into my allotted years. I think I was driven not be like my mother. That drive saw me move house every few years, change jobs and take up a new venture at the drop of a hat. What it didn't make up for was those lasting friendships others might have throughout their lives. My mother had one friend who died and her timidity stopped her making any more. I had tried to get her to extend herself. Perhaps she could join a group, start a book-club, find bingo. She made excuses and nothing transpired for my effort. It was always too hard to even try.

I always kept people at a safe ~ Christmas card distance. Now we had each other. If I thought about it, it would be the one opportunity to get to know my mother, and find out who the woman was. The dilemma would be what if I didn't like the woman I found.

The first weeks as I settled her in, showed her my life in small snippets and tried not to put her in a box, metaphorically and physically, I thought on how we would navigate the rest of her life. How do you fill the void? I could, I thought, just include her in my life. She'd become an appendage, like a handbag that goes everywhere. She would become a thing again. Or ... I could let her settle, like the sediment in a jar of pickles. She would gradually slip down and stay there, quiet and no trouble. She was accustomed to that sedentary type of life. She had never pushed herself. She'd never been driven. It was an appealing option.

I decided we would walk ... and talk.

I would get to know her, then I might make an informed decision on her future. And as we walked I would nurture her body and soul.

So I bought her some trainers, the first in her life that I could recall, and some comfy leggings. If we were going to walk, we needed to make the effort. I've been throwing myself into projects all my life, so my mother would be another project.

In thinking about my motives I might have come to the uncomfortable conclusion I was trying to make my mother happy. I was projecting my version of living onto the woman. She didn't complain.

But before we walked, my mother needed sustenance. She needed three meals a day. She needed a figurative and authentic chicken broth that would bring her back to life. I researched what older people need in the way of calorific content. I consulted with dieticians, doctors and bought supplements.

She didn't complain. I was taking control, just like my father had, since she had married at twenty, only this time I convinced myself I was keeping her alive. I wanted to nurture her body, as well as her soul.

'What would you like for lunch?' It was a simple question, but it threw my mother into a tizz. 'I'm not fussy.' She said it without so much as a twitch. It brought me back to my childhood so quickly I grabbed the shopping trolley for support. I'd heard those words all my life. I could smell the kitchen in the house I grew up in and see the meal being prepared on the kitchen sink. A feeling of stifling anxiety wove around my throat as I tried to concentrate on where I was in the moment. I felt the weight of the old house, the oppressive fug that invaded my everyday as I grew up. It was uncomfortable to be transported so effortlessly back to something I hadn't thought about in years. It makes you realise the things you carry with you all your life, just simmering beneath the surface, or put in a box and the lid shut, but they spring out when you least expect it. My mother had that power. She held the ignition switch to my childhood memories and without trying, could trigger everything I'd tried so hard to extinguish.

I admonished myself and told my inner psyche that I'd need to be on my guard. I would need to be ready for these sorts of occurrences. I needed a mechanism to rise above my childhood memories lest they catch up with me. So far I'd run fast enough for them to be left behind.

Not that I had a dreadful childhood. My mother and father, both in their twenties, did their best. Parents always do what they can, and fudge the rest. Children grow up not knowing anything is different in their small world. It is not until you see how the other half live that you begin to question what happens in your home. I saw other families having fun. I saw my cousins playing wonderfully rowdy cricket in the back yard. I watched the neighbours with an eagle eye, trying to work out why my family was different to theirs.

My childhood was fraught with the things unsaid, the silence of betrayal, the quiet of frustration. Ours was a house where no-one shouted.

When I bought home a report card it was never remarked upon. When I made my own clothes, there was never any astonishment at the quality. I learned early on never to ask, but wait. Sometimes what I hankered for never materialised.

I was seven and had an operation on my mouth. The treat was to be able to lie on the settee in the lounge room with my pillow and watch television. Then my father came home with a Barbie doll outfit. A gift out of the blue. I couldn't believe my luck. The memory stayed with me, a beacon of kindness I could call upon when I looked back, which wasn't often. We often remember the bad, rather than the good. I remember the silence, the pursed lips, the utter control of everyone. Everyone except my sister.

It was going to be a slow process to bring out the woman within. I wondered if we would be up for the challenge.

My mother stood in the supermarket aisle and looked at the food on offer.

'Salad?'

'If you like.'

I wanted to scream.

With a nourishing diet, my mother began to breathe again. Sometimes I felt she'd been holding her breath her whole life. Her cheeks filled out, her hair began to shine and she put on weight for the first time in years.

If I had to spoon feed the woman back to health, I would just do it. It wasn't hard to organise her calories, or get her to eat. It was hard to know if she appreciated the change as she did everything with the same modicum of emotion. It was like she was dead inside. I could understand she was going through the grieving process, a silent creeping canker that might eat your insides slowly, painfully, until its evil fills your every waking hour. Our family knew all about the process of grief. My sister was the cause.

My sister was the devil or the antidote to our family's dynamic. She made the noise when there was a void. She was the wind in our still world. She blew herself out one summer afternoon. One moment, and the world stopped spinning the way it always had. It might have been different if she'd walked out slamming the back door, like she always did. It might have made more sense if she'd been angry. But she left that day with a smile, a kiss for my mother and a hug for me. She was just going to the shops. Why she hugged me and kissed my mother I will never understand, but she left us with love, and got knocked down crossing the road.

We went through the motions of what people do in the circumstances. My father pursed his lips a little tighter, my mother dusted the venetian blinds and we carried on. My sister haunted the silent house. I longed for a slammed door, a whistle in the bathroom or a whirlwind of mess in the kitchen. I wanted to smell a cigarette in the toilet, a rum bottle hidden behind the water heater. She left a silence that was every bit as destructive as cancer.

My mother has regular visits to the doctor, but I couldn't say why. He'd look her over, pronounce her fit and issue a prescription for a pill. I expected him to say how well she looked, how amazed at her transformation he was, but perhaps he was too skilled for the flattery I felt I needed. My efforts didn't need affirming. He knew I was doing all that was required.

'I'm going to start walking.' My mother said it with a tiny bit of determination. Her doctor nodded. I so wanted to tell him it was my idea. I really wanted to explain my rationale, that it was cathartic ... for both of us, but I didn't. I think he knew the reason anyway.

Walking is one of those things that seems so natural, so right, it doesn't need anything else to make it perfect.

I picked out an easy route around the neighbourhood, something to see along the way and a circular course so we didn't need to backtrack. We would start on a Monday.

I had to stop myself from tying my mother's laces as I waited. She was becoming dependent upon me, and I was smothering her. The co-dependency was starting to grate my sensibilities. I was a vital, independent woman. I didn't need to feel virtuous or super charitable to validate my life.

Our walk started with me talking and her listening. We set an easy pace, almost a stroll as I pointed out houses, their time periods, their garden efforts and the history of the district. My mother listened, pointed out a bush or a flower she remembered from her youth and then it was over.

We did it again the next day, and every day for a month. Our times were getting shorter as her fitness improved. And we stopped talking. There was nothing to talk about. My mother didn't read the paper with any great insight. She didn't follow sport, or have a hobby. I could have asked her the difficult questions. I might have talked about her feelings, but my family didn't do that. We never had. An unwritten rule.

Then, one morning she talked about her childhood. It was just a prickle in her sock, but it opened the box of memories for her. I had heard some of her childhood from her brother, my uncle, but this day she took me back.

It was a moment that changed everything. I heard about my grandparents as young parents. She told me about the room she shared with her sister, the dog she had, the shoes she wore for her first day of school. I loved it all. It was all new to me and filled in the gaps of the family history.

Then she stopped almost mid stride and looked around.

'Where are we?'

'Just almost home.' I assumed she'd been so engrossed with her memories she's just become disorientated.

And she laughed. 'Of course.'

It was gratifying to see my mother's health return, all thanks to my efforts. A feeling of vindication and self-satisfaction is one chalked up on the board of life. I had achieved what I set out to do. My mother's physical wellbeing was coming up to par. Her doctor could not help but notice the difference, still he never remarked on it.

We began to walk further, and as we did, the walks were a trigger for my mother to slip into her childhood. I listened at first with fascination, then with a growing unease. The stories were getting complicated, convoluted and fanciful.

'Where are we?' she asked almost every day as we turned the corner at the gangster house and neared home.

I wanted to ask her before it was too late. I needed to know, but didn't know how to say it. In the end I rang my uncle. He wasn't certain, but that was enough. The word dementia was out in the open. It could never be put back in the box.

$$\underline{\qquad} \, \text{♫} \, \underline{\qquad}$$

4

I imagined the brain like a matrix of boxes. When we are young the boxes get filled with life. We can open them, close them and organise them. As we age we shut the boxes we don't need and archive them, sometimes never to be called upon again.

My mother's brain was archiving some boxes while she still needed them. There would be blank, black spots in her matrix. Her doctor said things like brain stimulation, exercise and looked at me to add,

'Love.'

The word held so much weight. So many expectations, so many emotions. It clung to me. It tattooed itself on my heart. I made an off the cuff remark, a failsafe switch when the going gets tough, and laughed. I don't think I was fooling him for one minute. I think he was too clever for that.

'Did you hear what he said?'

My mother nodded. I sat next to her in the car and I wondered what she felt. I almost held her hand. I felt gutted.

My project had just moved the goal posts. Somewhere along the line, sitting in the sun, drinking tea or gin and tonics, talking about life as we watch the sun go down, my fantasy had blown up in my face. There would never be the hoped for end of life closeness, the mother/daughter bond. My mother would move away gradually into a world of her own making. She would retreat from me to the march of her own drum. I could only watch.

'Are ... are you ok?' The woman sitting next to me in my car had shrunk. Her lucid moment at the Doctors was peppered with bad news. I couldn't put myself in her place. I couldn't imagine how she must feel. To lose your husband was one thing. To lose yourself over time was unthinkable. How do you process that information. To just fade away. All that you are just disappears and the worst of it is you can't remember. I felt numb, she must have felt bereft.

'Where are we?'

'At the beginning,' I said.

I watched my mother like a devotee watches their particular God for a sign. Her every move was calculated by me into a scale of one to ten. When she dropped a spoon, I wrote it down in my diary. When she made a mistake with the hot water, I noted it. That missed step, the search for the right word, I catalogued it all. She fell into depression and I couldn't blame her. I wasn't equipped to deal with her mental anguish, so I threw myself into study about dementia, the cause, the effect, the treatments, the scale of hope. I was doing something, although it seemed miniscule in comparison to the mountain we were about to climb.

Her life would need a re-evaluation. My life would need a paradigm shift. I shifted into high gear as my mother began to settle in the pickle jar.

She didn't need much. She ate, she slept, we walked and talked. As the days were crossed off she emerged from the diagnosis with a fatality that scared me. She had little left in her life and that small slither would be taken away. Why bother? Why bother indeed?

I got her into the kitchen. I set a task each day for her. She must be made to feel useful, vital, wanted, the experts said. I made lists. I crossed off jobs to be done and she revived and developed an appetite. There would be bites out of apples, half eaten biscuits stuffed down the side of the settee and crumbs in the bed. I didn't want to be a nag, after all, she was probably suffering, her mental anguish keeping her off kilter. I quietly suggested she eat at the table all the while making sure I didn't sound like her. My childhood was peppered with looks, evidence presented and a click of the tongue. I felt I was always a disappointment, no matter how much I tried to please.

We have an aversion to becoming our mothers. There is always the secret promise as we grow into women in our own right, that we will never be like our mothers. Yet, their words often slip from our lips. Their mores and values circle our arguments and their mannerisms cling to us despite our best efforts. I tried very hard not to emulate her, and pursed my lips a little tighter.

I would catch her eating from the fridge at any time of the day or night. It was very hard not to scold her, my mother's words on my tongue, our roles reversed.

So, in a grand, magnanimous gesture, I suggested we walked off the calories. I would look the other way when I found the evidence of her misdemeanors. I bought healthy snacks and left them around the house. It became a game of wits as I took control of her wellbeing. She became adept at sneaking and hoarding. I'd find food stuffed all over the place. It was a silent war of attrition. The war took me back to my childhood and we slipped effortlessly into the world we had inhabited in my youth. A world where nothing is said, but everything is understood. It ended in tears one afternoon when she couldn't open a packet of nuts.

'You're trying to poison me.' She threw the packet down and began to cry.

'What?' I offered her a box of tissues, but she pushed them away.

'I hate you.' I reached for the door. This wasn't what I envisaged when I signed up. She plopped down on the settee and stared into the void and I resisted the urge to run.

'Shall we go for a walk?' We'd only just come back, but I needed to get out, see the world, reacquaint myself with reality.

'A walk?'

'Yes.'

We reversed our route and everything was new again. I made a note to put the nuts in a jar.

She was watching television one late afternoon when a show came on that would have been more appropriate for after midnight. A couple were 'doing what they do on the discovery channel' albeit under the sheets. I rushed over and changed channels. I can't say why I was censoring her viewing, except our roles were so thoroughly reversed it just seemed like the right thing to do.

'I have had sex you know.' She frowned and pursed her lips.

What do you say to your mother at such a time?

'Well, obviously.' I made a glib remark.

'We were at it like rabbits.' I couldn't imagine my parents 'at it like rabbits'. I didn't want to imagine my parents at it like rabbits. Thinking about ones parents having sex is like an extreme sport. Not for the faint-hearted.

'Do you want a cup of tea?' I was struggling with the conversation.

I studied her as she watched the television. How much of her, of the mother I knew, was present at this moment in time? She looked clear, lucid, articulate. She looked like she knew what she was saying.

'Coffee maybe?' I wanted to be somewhere else.

'We were trying hard for your sister. We were practically hanging off the chandelier.'

'I'll put the kettle on.'

'You wouldn't know about that,' she said. I let the remark slide. I had decided I didn't want children quite early in life. It was a choice that fitted with my lifestyle. Some women don't feel the urge. Some women were different and it takes all sorts to make

24

up the milieu of life. It was rhetoric I had perfected over my years as an intelligent, vital, fulfilled woman.

'We weren't like young people today. Some of those women have had more than one. Elizabeth Taylor had eight. That's just legalised prostitution.' Her lips went to a sneer.

My mother the moralist. I watched for any forecast of fog descending over her, any twitch or missed word. It looked to me like she was in control. It looked like she knew just exactly what she was saying.

'We were in for life. Your father and I were devoted to one another.' She looked at me with a clear understanding of her motives.

'Nearly sixty years,' I said in the hope of steering the conversation in another direction.

'You can't even keep a man for two.' She studied the show on television, some banal game show with flashing lights.

How could the woman just drop that in my lap and walk away. It was a cruel gibe. I'd had a few relationships that never went anywhere and then one that lasted, until it didn't. When did my mother learn such cruelty, such bile. You can convince yourself of most things, but hurtful vitriol is hard to rationalise, even with the mother of all excuses, dementia. Everything she said might have a morsel of truth behind it. Is this what my mother thought of me? I tried hard to move on from her scorn, but once said, it can never be unsaid. I think that is why the truth hurts so much, because it can never be taken back.

It was as I was vacuuming up some nuts that she plopped into a chair and watched me.

'I had one of those.' She pointed to the vacuum cleaner. 'Your father gave it to me right after we were married.'

It was a fabrication. The brand hadn't been invented until the 1980s.

'Really?'

'Oh yes,' she said. I heard about the wrapping paper and the card. She explained she didn't know what it could be as they'd only just be married in the 1940s. She said it was the same as mine.

My mother had an alternative reality. I wondered briefly should I point out the obvious facts, discredit her memory. I decided to play along, after all, what harm could come of validating her belief. It was just a glitch in her matrix.

After the vacuum cleaner it was the ipad. My father had apparently given it to her on their first wedding anniversary. He knew they couldn't afford it, but he spent all their money on it.

26

The truth was the ipad was my idea. I schooled my father in its usefulness when he saw mine, and he lashed out a few years before he died. He played crosswords and word-search on it. I set him up with a few apps and it kept him occupied. My mother was convinced of her matrix memory.

'Where is it now?'

'Oh, I sold it.'

The truth was much more painful. She'd broken it when my father died. I had my suspicions that it wasn't an accident. As my father retreated into pain, the ipad was a quiet solace, preferable to my mother. It took his last days, rather than interact with his wife.

Where my mother dredged up these invented stories, I didn't know. Her brain was rewiring itself and creating new and original memories. It was scary and intriguing to watch.

There were still many more of the lucid days than glitches. Her eyes would glaze and the learned behaviours would kick in. I began to see a change in her face, her complexion and her stance when she was in the matrix. Her usual hunched self, with eyes that didn't quite see the world would be gone to be replaced with a self-assuredness that I'd never seen. She'd sit up straight, eat with gusto, engage in conversation, albeit ridiculously outrageous. I began to like the latter rather than the former and could read the signs. Here was a woman that looked like she could have some life, some fun.

Perhaps, this was my mother. Perhaps this was the woman who had been hiding all her life in my father's shadow, afraid to step out into the sunshine.

With her inhibitions gone, archived and forgotten she could be the woman she might have been. I'm not naïve enough to dismiss the thought that unshackled from my father, my mother found a life, albeit at the hands of a creeping disease. It was a cruel twist of fate.

When she was in the matrix it was a great temptation to exploit the moment. I wouldn't be human if I didn't have the thought that this was my chance to talk of things that never got an airing around the kitchen table. Maybe there would be a modicum of truth in the yarn she might spin. Perhaps dementia was a bit of a truth serum.

When you have an opportunity like this, there is a lot to think about. I would need to pick my moment. The conscience can be a great leveller. Would it be abuse to prise open one of my mother's boxes in the hope of finding the truth. Would I hurt her irrevocably for my own purpose? Was I being selfish? The word love, that had been tattooed on my heart by the doctor came back to taunt me. I might need to live with my culpability all my life. But then, I might destroy the mother I grew up with and replace her with someone I quite liked. I watched and waited. She might give me a morsel of her own accord.

We walked every day, and she talked her way around six kilometres. I heard about the war years, her years as a secretary and her time as a model for Vogue magazine.

'What!'

'Oh, yes.'

It was a hilarious moment, but I couldn't laugh because I had an idea.

$$\underline{\qquad} \, ♫ \, \underline{\qquad}$$
5

Just perhaps my mother had unfulfilled aspirations. Perhaps she wanted to be a model when she was young? It was the first I'd heard of it, but that wasn't surprising.

And so, I would make it happen. I was a photographer. I could do a shoot with my mother as the model. I knew people in the business of make-believe.

I threw myself into the project. Throwing myself into things was how I navigated the world. If you are busy there is no time for anything else. I didn't need to contemplate my lack of relationships, my boundless energy for independence. This was how I operated.

My mother believed she was a model and now she would have the photographic memories to prove it.

There was the hair, the makeup, the dresses. A gorgeous organza dress in russet and orange was made, the shoes provided by wardrobe. She had day wear, cocktail wear and evening wear. My organisational skills kicked in and our shoot was scheduled for an early morning start on the Wednesday. My crew were energised by the idea and volunteered their time. The mood was set on high as they pampered and preened my mother, playing along with her fantasy. Make believe came naturally to these people, they did it for a living. My mother lapped it up.

We took over the train station platform for an hour and I shot my mother in all her wonderful glory. She looked gorgeous. She posed. She pouted. She swished her handbag and hat about like a professional. It was a day to remember. I hoped she would remember.

I bound the photographs into a portfolio, added a mock-up of a vogue magazine cover and left them on our kitchen table and waited. My mother was a star. She recognised herself, made the memory stick and became a model. This was something I could do for her.

As we walked we talked about her photoshoot. I heard about her career of modelling and how she didn't regret a thing, because that was how she met my father. It was all woven into the threads. She had the whole story in her mind and compartmentalised.

What we had done was fill a box with a memory. Only this time she had a portfolio to prove it.

I'd catch her looking at the pictures, sometimes with a frown on her forehead. When my lucid mother was in residence she'd narrow her eyes and stare at the pictures, I imagined, willing her brain to marry them with her reality. She'd trace over the dresses with her finger and read the words on the mock magazine.
'I had fun didn't I?'
'Yes, you certainly did.'

I was still watching for a moment when I might pry open a box and it came one morning as we were walking and it started to rain. We dashed for the shelter of a tree and my mother began to giggle.
'What's so funny?'
'Well, do you remember when your sister put the hose on the roof?'
It was a memory that popped up when I heard dripping water too. My sister had climbed the roof of the garage and planted the sprinkler on top, so we could have rain and try out our new raincoats.
'Yes, I remember,' I said.
'She was always like that you know, right

from the start.'

'The start?'

'Born with a twinkle in her eye. A nose for mischief.'

'Do you miss her?'

'Every day.'

It was the most my mother had said to me, about my sister, in my lifetime. I looked at her and saw a tear mingle with the rain.

'The best time to cry is in the rain,' she said.

'Yes. I know.'

As with all things in life, we settled into a routine. It wasn't just the physical things, but we laid down the unwritten rules for what we would and would not say to each other. And gradually the same stifling feeling I had had as a child crept into my life. There didn't need to be any list, nothing written down to know where the line in the sand was. We'd been living with the knowledge all our lives, so it was an easy slide.

We would walk, sometimes talk, sometimes just pound the footpath in our own thoughts. I'd often look at my mother when she was sitting in the sun, reading a book or staring into space. What went on inside her head. Was there anything going on at all?

And as she settled in the pickle jar, I began

to resent her intrusion into my world.

It was just the small things at first. Nothing I could really complain about when people all over the world had it worse than me. But those little things niggled me like that prickle in her sock. They brought up memories of why I bolted from the house of my parents as soon as I saved a kitty. It was the total compliance, the lack of verve that got under my skin. No matter how hard you try to be nice, to be accommodating and pleasant, behind it all there is a feeling that it's not quite right. My mother had her finger on my ignition switch. Whether she knew it or not. I became jumpy and avoided anything that might be a trigger. I'd talk about the weather, the television, the lateness of the post, anything rather than feel the oppression of nothingness my mother carried around with her.

'Do you want to do something?' I had scheduled three days to go somewhere, see something.

'Whatever you want to do.'

'No. Don't pull that with me.' It fell out of my mouth before I had time to hold back. My apology was on my lips, but I couldn't say it. She looked at me and pulled the ignition switch. I felt like a teenager yelling at my mother. It felt horrible. It felt like I was not in control.

'I'll leave it up to you.' It came out of her mouth like a bomb. I wanted to shake her. Grab her and tell her that life isn't like that. We all need to make decisions in our lives. We can't always leave it to someone else. Sometimes there isn't an easy option.

'For God's sake.' I threw up my hands. 'What do you fucking want.'

Then she went for my throat. 'I don't want to be a burden,' she said.

The punch of those words went right to my guts. Here was a woman thrown into something she had no choice over. No-one had asked her would she like to live with me. No-one had listened to her. She was just a passenger of her own life.

She sat at the table and smoothed the placemat, over and over. There was, it looked to me, nothing else in her life. She had nothing to fall back on.

I had a lifetime of experiences. I had a joy of living that took me to happy places. Concerts, exhibitions, travel, people, jobs. I knew it was almost a mania to do things, like a junkie getting their next fix. But I had a life I liked and understood. What did this woman have, sitting at my table?

'Did you ever ...' I began then stopped.

The rule book between us prevented me asking that question. The apology didn't come, instead I asked,

'What would you and dad have done with three days?'

She looked at me.

Of course I knew the answer. My father would organise something, book the hotel room, gather the pamphlets and fill the car with petrol. My mother was just a passenger.

On our school holidays, we were never told where we were going, it all just happened. We were never asked our opinion, and perhaps in those distant days children weren't consulted. We were just put in the car; our mother packed our bags and we arrived somewhere else. We didn't ask, what would be the point, there was no going back.

'Shall we go to Cockle Bay?'

Our family often went to Cockle Bay. I knew if my father took the North Road and then a left onto the coast road we were probably headed to Cockle Bay. I'd take long solitary walks along the beach, collecting shells. My sister preferred the main street.

'That sounds good.' She said it in a tiny voice, and I watched a tear escape from the corner of her eye. It might have been the moment to say all that I felt about our situation. How being thrown together was

36

going to be hard for both of us. How I didn't like her triggers to my past and what I hoped for our future. I put the kettle on instead.

It was on our first morning walking along the main street of the Bay that we stopped and looked into the window of the newsagents. In France it is lèche vitrine, licking the glass. I've always liked to lick the glass. It is the promise of nice things, the expectations and the fun of knowing you'd never buy it in a million years. We looked at the display of pens and pencils.

'Let's go in.'

My mother was drawn to the coloured pencils. She began with a story about pencils. An inventive tale that took a good ten minutes.

'Would you like some?'

'Oh, yes please.'

It took a moment to process the delight in her voice. She sounded excited. I knew it wasn't my mother talking, rather the matrix glitch, but it lightened my day. We bought a Derwent set of pencils and three colouring-in books. The joy in her eyes was enough for me. She couldn't wait to get back to our rented shack on the beach to start.

Oh how I wished this woman was my mother. I could really like someone like her.

Our three days were spent in walking, collecting shells and eating out. My mother ate things she never ate. She had fish. She had avocado. She asked for a beer. I had never seen my mother drink alcohol. She was a fiery teetotaller. My father might indulge once a year at a Christmas party, but our house was dry. My sister didn't agree with the house rules and broke them every chance she could. I could take it or leave it and for the most part left it.

'Oh, I've always had a beer when your father had one.'

'Naturally.'

'It's good for the blood.'

'Of course.'

And so it went.

She concocted stories for three days. It was then I decided to write some of them down. We'd walk in the morning, collect our bakery treats for morning tea and then settle in until lunch. She'd talk and colour-in, and I'd write. I'd put on some music in the afternoon and we'd read, nap and get ready for our meal out. It was relaxing. I knew I was only babysitting, but it felt good just to do as little as possible.

My mother was dedicated to her craft of colouring-in. She really enjoyed it. I wondered who was enjoying it, my mother or the glitch. But what did it matter. All I was trying to do was make her happy. Isn't that what we all try to do in the end, make someone happy?

The anniversary of my father's death crept up on us while we were doing other things. I'd not thought about him for most of the year and it was only the anniversary that prompted the mental guilt of neglect. Why I didn't think about him, I put down to my mother. Not that I needed an excuse, but she was conveniently available. His presence settled over the house and we took up our familiar stations. She shrank and I sulked, then I decided to go away.

Going away entailed finding someone or some place to deposit my mother. There is another world that the able bodied don't see. We don't know how those with less acuity navigate the world. Now I was plunged into that world.

I filled in forms. I gave details. I made lists. And at the end of it all, it was the department that decided when I should go, not me. I was allotted a slot of four days when my mother would be taken care of in a *wonderfully stimulating environment nestled in the hills with panoramic views'*. They boasted fresh air, fine food and a price to match. I persuaded myself I needed four days to ... There was no plan, aside from a small photographic job I had convinced myself I needed to do. I packed my mother's bag, drove to the hill retreat and settled her into her small room.

'Are you coming back?'

God, how do you answer that. What must she think of me if she is willing to believe I'm abandoning her.

'Of course.'

I watched from the tea station as she was led to the communal lounge. She had her colouring-in bag with her, but she looked lost, frightened, out of touch. Then, before I had a chance to rescue her a woman came over and grabbed her pencils.

'Oh, take them. I used to paint in oils.' My mother, under stress, became someone else. I hoped she would stay that way until I picked her up on the Friday. My mother, the life and soul of the party.

I flew to my friend's house and the life I once had before my mother. I indulged in all the things I once did to the point of exhaustion, until my friend sat me down with a glass of wine and said,

'Just stop.'

I knew. I knew what he was telling me. It was a small epiphany of sorts. And then I let it all out. The frustration, the wracking guilt, my father, the realisation that he probably killed my mother years ago. My eagerness to make things right. I said I was keeping her stories. He listened. He poured the wine. He had an idea.

♫

6

Four days felt like a six week break. I had read that people can burn out if they don't have the skills to care for someone 24/7.

'It's not a holiday for her.' The nurse packed my mother's bag and kept her eyes down. She had probably seen this scenario many times.

'I know that.'

'It's her life.'

Had I been trying to be the tourist guide for my mother over the year.

'If you look to your left ...' I tried so hard to fill her every waking hour with something. It had kept me occupied, and perhaps that was my raison d'être.

'I need guidance.'

A group was recommended. There would be a crèche of sorts for our charges and we could learn how to be a better version of ourselves. Just belonging might be the strength one needs to navigate the new reality.

I've never been a great joiner. I hate to be

corralled, or judged. But the first step was to say this wasn't for me, it was for my mother.

And the first question they asked was,

'Are you angry?'

Of course we were all angry. Our lives were completely taken over by someone else. Sometimes by someone else we didn't particularly like. Who wouldn't be angry.

'What keeps you doing it?'

These were hard questions. They are the sort of questions that make you squirm in your seat or run away.

But we listened. We took comfort in the fact that we were doing something, rather than nothing and leaving our relatives to the dismal 'system'. And I gradually began to navigate to a place where I could be comfortable. My group became a support and an ally. We needed each other if only to validate our decisions.

My mother liked her outing. She'd sit around the table and regale her companions with her life.

'Your mother is pretty amazing.' The woman in charge said.

'I know.'

Our home life was a little better. I let my mother relax and I took a step back and kept listening to her amazing life.

'Are you sure?' I asked.

'Oh yes, I've done it hundreds of times.' My mother was so assured of her memory who was I to disagree.

And that was how my friend's bright idea began.

We caught a plane to the Great Barrier Reef for a week away. I had a photographic assignment, but nothing that might take me from my care duties. It was for a brochure and included a freebie, a trip on a boat.

My mother hates boats. She always maintained she gets sea sick in the bath. I looked at her as the woman asked would we be taking up the offer.

'We're going on a boat,' I said. She looked at me and smiled.

'You love boats.' I waited for the words to sink in.

'Yes, I love boats. I've been on boats all my life. Hundreds of times.'

'Yes, we will take your freebie.'

Auto suggestion can be a powerful tool, or an instrument of torture. My mother convinced herself not only that she loved boats, but she practically lived on them in her youth. Was I being manipulative or practical.
 44

Or, just maybe I was giving my mother a small taste of the life she never had.

It wasn't particularly rough going to the docking station on the reef. I watched my mother for any sign of anxiety. She seemed to be enjoying herself. I took some photographs of her having a good time. My friend had suggested I keep a scrapbook of her adventures. Memory joggers, he called them.

She ate her sandwich with a beer in one hand. Was this the woman who couldn't look at a boat without feeling sick? Was this even my mother?

When we arrived at the dock, people got in the water to snorkel. My mother never swims. She hates water on her face and rarely gets under the full force of a shower. Now she was lining up for flippers, goggles and snorkel.

'Are you sure?' I asked.

'Oh, don't worry about me. I'm like a fish.' There is just so much derring-do an old woman can do before you start to think about safety. My mother couldn't swim. I'd never seen her in the sea in my life.

I knew she was fit enough, healthy enough because I'd been the one to take care of her.

They give the non-swimmers, the timid and the old a floaty noodle and life jacket.

45

I took pictures as she plopped in the water and smiled. I waved. She waved back and laughed. And isn't the point of life to be happy. My mother was happy.

'I saw a fish,' she yelled at me. I liked this other woman. I liked her a lot.

We spent our time eating out, trying new exotic dishes and watching the sun go down. The only snag was, I was doing it with the glitch in the matrix. As children we often wish we had a mother like our friends mother. Well, I did anyway. I would see them in the kitchen, laughing, talking, handing out biscuits. I craved that sort of mother. Now I had her.

'You can't make me.' She said it with a force I didn't think possible. There were tears in her eyes as she stood her ground at the airport. People stared. I wanted to shout at them to mind their own bloody business, but also to explain that my mother had dementia. I whispered to the attendant and we were ushered into the boarding tunnel.

'She's taking me away.' My mother jabbed her finger at me. 'She's leaving me.'

Obviously I wasn't, but the attendant couldn't board us with my mother in a state of distress.

46

I offered a beer which only infuriated my mother. She began to berate me as if I was my sister.

'You will be in trouble when your father finds out. Your sister may be dull as ditch water, but she never drinks.' I swallowed the hurt, the anger at the words. I knew logically it wasn't my mother talking, it was the matrix, but once the words are out they can never be put back. It would be something I would try to forget.

My support group had recounted this behaviour in their charges. We all commiserated while saying a silent prayer that it never happen to us. The group were taught how to de-escalate the situation. I put my study into practice. There were tears, tugging, pulling and nasty words I never thought I'd hear my mother say. Where did she learn how to swear?

It was after a colouring-in book was offered that she took a deep breath.

'It's all I ever wanted,' she said. If only that were true.

When we were settled back into our routine at home I compiled our photographs and put them in a portfolio for her to peruse. Then, I put them on-line on my web page. They were good examples of what I could do.

I added a small snippet of a story, chronicling my mother's new life, one that fate had dealt.

The fashion model was now practically a mermaid. I began to take photos of her around the house. Her pensive moods, her sheer joy at finding just the right colour of pencil for her pictures and her face while she slept. She had an innocence when she slept, like all the things the world put on us is taken away with sleep. Her face was confusion free, at peace.

I made a compendium of my mother on my web page. It was a study of a woman I was beginning to know. Her portraits made more sense to me than words or memories.

We walked, we went to the group, we shopped and I think she was happy. Her lucid moments were now becoming dangerous territory as she started to cry, often. I think she knew what was happening, how her brain was archiving her memories, the ones she needed most, to be who she was, and it hurt. Her moments of clarity were like slow torture. How do you rationalise your demise, when you know you will gradually be rubbed out, fade away like a photograph left in the sun. Everything that you are relies on who you were and how you shaped your life. To have that dissolve and know it is inevitable is

48

a huge burden to shoulder. And I could only watch.

Once or twice she thought I was my sister, and that hurt. She'd look at me with a scowl, then a frown and say,

'I don't know what your father will say when he finds out.' I knew she was talking about my sister, as I'd never been subjected to that rhetoric. I was the dutiful one. I never caused a fuss. I was 'dull as ditch water'.

I began to dread the lucid moments. I didn't know what to say. I hadn't been brought up in a house where we beat our chests and beared our soul. My mother was looking for a way out of the labyrinth of confusion, and I couldn't even hold her hand. We weren't a demonstrative family. There was the inevitable confusion that could bring her to howling cries of frustration.

She would rage at a blouse that wouldn't button or a word that refused to present itself.

'Just call it an eggbeater,' I offered. Even that safe word was forgotten at times and it invariably ended in tears.

She poured over her portfolio of photographs, conjuring up new and exciting stories about her adventures. It was early evening and we were relaxing with a wine, (she now drank wine) and she said,

'I remember when I went on a zip line across that gorge.'

'A zip line? Are you sure?'

I couldn't imagine how that thought got in to the matrix, but she was clear on the details.

'Oh, yes. Done it hundreds of times.'

It didn't take more than a day to find a zip line that was safe for all skill levels and a tourist attraction. We drove up the valley to a themed village of the 1800s and parked the car.

'Don't leave me will you?' my mother said.

'I promise.' I kept a tight hold on the steering wheel and looked straight ahead. The ignition switch turned on a memory of my sister saying the same words. We were lying in the warm sand at the beach and she reached over to grab my hand. We were only 12 and 15 years old. I, at 12 wasn't planning to go anywhere just yet. I had a map of the world on my wall, but it was just for lèche vitrine. I can remember that moment with a lucidity that brings it into sharp focus. My sister was always the one to grab my hand, pat me on the back, pull my hair or hug me. She was made of different cloth to the rest of us. I often play the moment back. It makes me feel close to her, it makes me feel human.

The zip line was an easy ride in a harness. I explained that my mother wanted one last thrill, and the staff were super obliging. My mother didn't like heights. She'd take the lift rather than the escalators. I'd never seen her extend herself over the edge, metaphorically or physically. This adventure was a gamble for both of us. I wanted her to be happy and she needed a memory.

Her face was one of expectation. I eagle eyed her for any sign that this was a mistake on my part, but her visage was clear, excited and untroubled. My other mother was having a ball. She revelled in the attention, flirted with the attendants and cracked a joke. When did my mother ever crack a joke?

'Ready?' I asked. She nodded and gave me a thumbs up. This dare devil person was the antonym to the mother I knew. She hit the ignition switch with her smile and I was about eight years old, wishing that I had a mother like my girlfriend's mother. At that young age I even took to praying for a miracle. It didn't take long to come to the conclusion that there was no man with a white flowing beard waiting to grant me something to make my life complete.

They say be careful what you wish for. Had I created something I wanted without knowing it? And now the question was, did I want my real mother back?

They strapped her in for the ride of her life and I took the photographic evidence. We did it twice for the price. People were fascinated that an older woman was game for fun.

'That's my mother.' I said it with pride, although I knew in truth that it wasn't who she really was, but just a glitch.

'It's just like parachuting isn't it?' my mother said, grinning.

I went on line to look for skydiving.

♫

7

Something like an older woman on a zip line gets a lot of traction on the internet. Our trip to the valley started to snowball.

The first I head of it was from a friend. She emailed me that she'd seen a woman on a zip line and wasn't it a terrific boost to know when we also get old we can still do things like that. I pointed out that I had good genes as the woman in question was my mother. The snowball effect quickened its pace as my friend also happen to work in radio.

The interview was set up via a zoom connection and I stipulated I'd like some sort of agenda. I didn't want the whole thing to go off on a tangent of dementia care, Government spending for the disabled and other difficult pills to swallow.

Honestly, I didn't see a problem in showing older people doing things. We all have different lives to live. If my pictures spur just one other older woman to take the plunge, and do something, then the interview would be worth it.

My mother sat by my side, and we logged on.

'I'm not crazy you know,' she said to me as we waited to be filtered into the intro.

'I know that.' I tried to gauge how lucid she was or how far she might slip into the matrix. She'd become adept at hiding her facial expressions. Over the year it had become noticeable to me, and I presumed the doctor. She'd put on a telephone voice and look interested in what you were saying, or telling her. She'd cock her head to one side like a dog and nod. It took me a good while to recognise the ruse. I wondered if she was trying to hold onto the last vestiges of who she was, trying to fool herself - and everyone else. She wasn't fooling anyone.

Now she cocked her head and frowned.

'You don't need to say anything.'

'Oh, don't worry. I won't embarrass you.' It was said with a snip of venom. I wondered if I'd soon be dealing with three versions of my mother. First the swearing, now the sniping.

I was surprised at the response across the airwaves. People were calling in to congratulate my mother and I. We were challenging the stereotypical norms. We were an inspiration.

It was when I casually mentioned my mother's interest in a sky dive that the offer came through. Some company was giving us the chance of a lifetime. Of course it would be a big free advertising boost, but they couched it in terms of giving my mother her one big, lasting memory.

'And have you ever sky dived?' the interviewer asked my mother.

'Oh, yes, done it hundreds of times.'

They have a buddy system in the air. The passenger is strapped to someone else who holds all the strings. It sounded a lot like the perilous slide into caring for someone with dementia. I would stay on the ground, but the company assured me there would be plenty of photo opportunities.

'She's in good hands,' the skydiver said.

My mother laughed and pecked the man on the cheek. When had she become this brazen? When did my mother ever peck another man on the cheek?

As the plane took off, my mother waved and I wondered had I created something I couldn't put back in the box? Just a year ago she was a frail woman, one that couldn't turn a tap, and now she was a zip line, skydiver.

The whole affair was live streamed to the

control room and a copy would be available to take home. I watched my mother's eyes for any sign that I should abort the dive. Here was a woman who in her former life didn't drive, didn't like water on her face or heights, strapped to a man about to jump out of a plane.

'She's quite a woman, your mother.' The woman at the control centre watched the whole thing on her screen.

What do you say when someone only knows the derring-do. They didn't know my mother. I wondered if I knew her. Was this who she really was, who she really wanted to be?

They leapt into fresh air and I held my breath. She waved to the camera.

'At least she has all her own teeth,' I said. A glib answer in times of stress.

The jumpers were met at the gate by a television crew clamouring for a word from my mother. I hung back and watched.

'I'm not crazy you know.' She said it and it became a catch phrase.

It didn't take 24 hours and there was a t-shirt with the slogan emblazoned over the front.

I'm not crazy you know!

Old people were wearing the shirt within three days.

I pasted all the photos in her album and it became her 'go to' when she was my mother, the one I understood. The mother that didn't want to be a burden.

I passed on a morning television interview several times as I felt protective of her vulnerability. It's hard to ignore the clamour of fame - fleeting fame. I wasn't so crazy to believe that my mother would get more than Andy Warhol's touted 15 minutes.

We kept to our routine while the whirlwind of my mother's fame swirled in ever increasing circles.

Media outlets started using my photos without my permission. My mother was splashed over the talk shows in her organza extravaganza. Someone got hold of the Vogue mock-up and suddenly she was in demand for modelling. I ignored all the advances, the inducements and the promises. We were given things in the hope we'd promote them. It made me feel tawdry, shallow. If this was the price of fame, I didn't want it. Thankfully my mother was oblivious to most of the hype. She was in a fuddle just cleaning her teeth. If I had subjected her to all the wooing I dread to think what might happen.

I wanted a sense of normality, but more than that I wanted things to be back the way they were. I understood where the goal posts stood when I was in control. Things were getting out of my control. I feared the day someone might come snooping into our background and dredge up my father, my sister and suppose us just shysters out for a perceived gain. I'd seen that sort of thing happen and it could cut down a decent human being, tear them to shreds, just for being themselves. When the mob had you by the throat, there was no stopping them.

'That's a plucky woman.' My mother was watching the television and saw her skydiving exploits.

Her inability to recognise herself, her short term memory gone on this particular occasion, was a jolt. What was it all for, if not to make her happy. Something to look back on. Maybe she just needed to live in the moment. Maybe that would be enough?

I showed her the photos of her adventure and we talked over the event.

'Of course I remember,' she said. It was a lie. She had become increasing proficient at lying; for her benefit and mine.

The invitation came via a courier and big bunch of flowers.

'Is it my birthday?' We stood at the door and took the delivery.

'As a matter of fact it is.' If my mother was living in the moment then every day was her birthday.

'We need a cake.'

So we went shopping for a birthday cake of gaudy exuberance. I wrapped a few presents and we bought champagne.

'I've always liked champagne.'

'So you have.' I could play the game.

The invitation was from the people who do car racing on Mt Panorama. They were giving my dare-devil mother the chance to be a passenger in a V8 around the circuit. I couldn't imagine my mother in a racing car. She didn't drive. She clung to the seatbelt with white knuckles when we drove in the hills.

We were to be picked up in a limousine and treated like VIPs.

'Have you ever been in a limousine?'

'Oh yes, hundreds of times.'

The track was awash with VIPs. We were

just two of two dozen who were to have a crack at the race track. It was a gala event with catering.

'Is it my birthday?' My mother looked at the food, the people, the bunting.

'As a matter of fact it is.'

They kitted her out in a suit and helmet. Gopro cameras were positioned at every angle and she gave the thumbs up to the driver. I heard her over the headset they supplied.

'It's my birthday you know.'

Seeing your mother reach over 200km/h and become airborne is a heady feeling. I watched as her face registered fear, delight, and back to fear. Was the driver trying to hasten her journey to the other side by scaring her to death?

'They all do that.' The man at the console saw my face and read it like a book.

When it was over she was pulled out of the car like a pro and waited patiently for someone to take her helmet off. I rushed in to fuss over her, cursing myself as I undid the strap. I didn't want it to look like I wiped her nose and pulled her pants up after a toilet break. She was the woman of the hour, the woman who could conquer the world, one moment at a time. We were given photographs, hats, merchandise dripped from our elbows in fashionable bags. Was this what life was all about? It was a hard call.

We were driven home in the limo, drunk on the elixir of life. It was easy when you didn't need to do anything but be present. Of course her racing exploits were plastered over the television. She had three minutes at the end of every news bulletin. The called her remarkable, wonderful, an example of old age, a marvel. Every accolade was a fabricated lie. This woman who could do anything was not my mother. If you can't remember why you are afraid, you might just become fearless. I rationalised it with the only words that put some sense to it all. She was happy.

I tried to keep to normality. We walked. We went shopping, but she was being recognised whenever we ventured out. People would come up to her, expecting a word, a conversation, a smile.

Sometimes my mother would oblige, other times she'd become confused, agitated and lost for a word.

'I honestly didn't realise I had so many relatives.' She said it in the car as we were coming home from the shops. Who was I to tell her different.

'Big family,' I said.
'Yes.'

The notoriety of my mother grew. Her exploits were becoming legendary. And then we started to get the letters. They came forwarded by the radio, the television and my business email.

My father has dementia and your mother gives us such joy. To know that a woman can still participate in life.

You are a credit to everyone who has cared for a loved one with dementia.

Thank you. I feel better knowing that your mother can still partake in life. My husband has just been diagnosed with dementia.

There were hundreds of letters about my mother, my care for her, my love for her, my devotion. I felt a bit of a fraud.

We also got letters begging for help. Sign this petition, join our group, give us money. I stopped looking at my emails. Then I delisted. I left the boxes of letter at the back door. I wasn't equipped to deal with this sort of notoriety.

But it was the vitriol that cut into me.

I was abusing my mother for my own business. It was elder abuse. I should be ashamed at the way I profit from my mother.

These people didn't know me or my mother, but they felt they had a right and privilege to slander us, just because they had seen us on television. The outpouring of hate sapped my reserves. When attacked, it is natural to defend oneself. I wanted to write to every one of those hate letters and let them know that I was doing my best. I was doing something for my mother before she was archived. I wanted to explain to them that this was my one chance to get to know my mother. If that meant that every day was her birthday, then that's what it would take.

My group were split.

On the one hand, some thought my idea brilliant. They wished me every success, and all the luck in the world. They wished they had thought of it. They loved the idea that someone with dementia could still have fun. It gave them hope. It gave them the will to keep doing what they were doing, day after day, year after year.

'Who are you?' was a question these people dealt with on a daily basis. My mother kept them sane. Some of them began to wear the t-shirt and began to believe its message.

I'm not crazy you know!

My mother and I were the best feel good message they had, and they clung to that message like survivors to a raft.

The other camp sucked at our vitals. People who had listened to me. Some who had shared their stories now turned away. But as they turned they spat their resentment, their jealousy, their hate at my face.

We were giving the whole disease a bad name. Dementia wasn't a joke, or a fast car ride, it was a life sentence for the spouse, the carer, the mother or father. I was being exploitive of a woman who was incapable of making a decision of her own. I was abusing my mother and should be ashamed, reported. My mother should be taken from me and put in a home. They came at me with words that stung. They belittled my efforts. They dug into my feelings for my mother and ripped them up like a tickertape parade. I was a bad person. I wasn't fit to look after my mother.

I could have told them I didn't get any money for anything. I might have said I was just trying to make my mother happy. I pursed my lips a little tighter.

'Get away,' my friend suggested. He said he was headed overseas. We could use his apartment for a while. Incognito. It sounded a delicious word. The hydra of media would find some other news. We could get on with our lives.

'Don't leave me will you?'

'Never.' I strapped her into the airline seat and set her up with her book.

♪

8

We slipped into anonymity in the city and established a routine. Our walk would take us past familiar landmarks that could be found on any postcard. We went out to eat on alternate evenings, trying different cuisines and usually walked home.

The media found someone else to annoy, but every once in a while my mother would pop up as dementia was discussed. She was the gold standard on what might be achieved. I still took photos of her and pasted them in her scrap book.

She looked at the book less often, and I watched her more often. I could see a subtle change as my mother slowly disappeared.

It was a Tuesday and raining. We sat at the big picture window watching the scudding clouds, drinking tea when she turned to me.

'I never had a favourite you know.'

I knew what she meant. My sister always had the attention. She craved it, good or bad, yelling or cuddling. She took my parents time. I stayed in the background, in a world I made.

'Your sister just needed more of me. You were so self-contained, like you father.'

The moment was a gift.

'And I wanted to be so different,' I said.

We sat there watching the weather, our tea growing cold.

There were strings of days when my mother fell into a funk. She'd shrink into her bed and no matter how I tried to cajole her, she refused to get up.

'I need to go out,' I said. I had an assignment I needed to post.

'Well go.'

I couldn't just leave her in the apartment. The post office was a short three minute walk. I'd be back before she had time to put her slippers on. She hadn't got out of bed for hours.

I quietly slipped out of the door and raced.

And what everyone dreads, happened. I came back to an empty apartment.

Thinking logically she couldn't have gone far. I checked and all her shoes were still in the laundry. She was in slippers.

There was CCTV in the foyer. They would have her on tape.

'No, hasn't worked for a while now. Better ring the police.'

The female police officer was calm. I was anything but calm. It had been an hour and my mother was wandering a big city probably in pyjamas and fluffy slippers.

'You left her alone?'

'Well, I could have got a courier for the package, but I thought ... yes, I left her. For three minutes.'

'And what was she wearing.'

'I don't know.'

'And how long have you been caring for your mother.'

I just wanted them to scour the streets. Put out an all bulletin alert or whatever they did. I didn't need the questions, the look in her eye, the accusation that I wasn't doing my bit. The minutes ticked by as we waited for a call.

'You live here?'

'No.' I didn't need chit chat. I paced the room. The shadows lengthened as we waited.

There was a call on the officer's phone. She nodded. She looked at me and nodded again.

'Nothing.'

'Shit.' I grabbed my handbag and opened the front door to get out on the streets and start looking.

My mother was standing on the landing talking to the next door neighbour.

'Oh, hello.'

'What the fuck do you think you're doing.' It came out all wrong. I was angry. I was upset. The neighbour looked at my mother and then me. My mother began to cry and wiped her nose on her pyjama sleeve. I offered a tissue, but she shunned my appeasement.

'I thought you left.' She just managed to squeak out the words. I looked at her and saw something in her demeanour I hadn't seen before. There was something not quite right about the way she looked at me. It didn't feel ... I hunted for the word. It didn't feel genuine. My mother was playing to the gallery. The deceit was such a shock I took a step back from the situation.

'She just popped out and the door closed on her. I let her stay until we heard someone come back.

'Thanks.'

The police officer came out and assessed the whole scenario in a minute. She called it in and after I signed a paper, she left.

'She's that woman on the television, isn't she?' The neighbour raised his eyebrows.

'Umm.'

'I recognised her.'

'Yes. Thanks.' I pulled my mother inside

and shut the door.

'He's a nice man.' She calmly walked to the bedroom and shut her door. I had been played.

How do you get angry with someone when you are supposed to be caring for them. My group often discussed the frustration, the unfairness of the situation. We all had lives too, and this person was sapping at our vitals like aphid suck on a stem. They were needy, continually in our thoughts, always there.

I took a long slug of whisky and soda and practiced breathing deeply. Revenge is sweet because it feels like justice is served. The feeling of anger slowly subsided to be replaced with measured calm. This deceit, this lying was just another facet of my mother. It was if she was going through the seven deadly sins in three months. I felt incapable of carrying on. The group often talked about the feeling of helplessness. I prided myself that it would never happen to me. I was too much together. I had lists and plans. I had control of the situation.

Now my world was falling apart. How to navigate life with someone who doesn't understand reason, or logic would be too hard. I wasn't qualified to do this. I felt like giving up. How did people do it for year after year? They were the stars. They were all saints.

I decided we would go home.

♪

9

Back in my own environment I consulted her doctor. He was understanding and suggested day-care for my mother. She could go three days a week. It sounded like a plan.

We sat in the car and looked at the building. In it's previous life it must have been a three bedroom house. Now it was day-care for carers to have a break.

'Are you coming back?'

'Always.'

Inside there were people in bright aprons scattered throughout the rooms. It looked like kindergarten, not an adult centre for respite. I had expected book cases, tables and soft sofas. This was garish. It was institutional in the extreme.

'We don't get much funding.' The woman with Muppets on her apron showed me the toilet facilities. They had a variety of disabled people in the centre, some strapped into their chairs, others sitting at tables. The hills retreat was far superior, but too expensive and always fully booked.

'What will my mother do?'

'Oh, we have all sorts of activities.' The woman looked over my mother to me. 'She's the skydiver isn't she?'

'Hmm.' I didn't like it. I'd packed my mother's lunch, her books, her colouring-in, but the place gave me the creeps.

'Sorry. I don't think ...' I shrugged.

I hustled my mother out of the place and when we sat in the car I gave her a high five. We had escaped.

'That was a close call,' I said. 'Have you ever been ten pin bowling?'

'Oh, yes. Hundreds of times.'

I hadn't been bowling since I was a kid. We sat in the booth and ate her sushi and sandwiches. She had no idea on how to bowl, but it was fun. We pulled in a few kids that were hanging around and spent the morning having a ball. I took some photos of the gang. It felt good just to be normal. I'd never done stuff with my mother. We never had that connection. She taught me to knit when I was seven, but that was it.

'Did you have a good time?'

'Oh yes.' She sat in the car and looked straight ahead. I couldn't quite tell if she really knew how to process the question. It would take a moment to evaluate good versus not so good. What constitutes a good time?

She was in such a good mood that I felt in a good mood too, so I ventured to ask,

'Are you happy mum?'

'Oh yes.' Her eyes shone with something that was fleeting. I might call it love, but that word had so many variations. It was a contentment, an ease with living. My mother was happy.

I decided that evening to plan one *adventure before dementia* a week. We'd pick somewhere where we'd never been and just get out there and do it. I would work from home and if we needed extra care, then I'd pay for a day nurse at home. I wondered why I didn't think of it before. Trying to keep all the balls in the air had nearly killed me.

The agency sent around a woman who looked like she could cope with anything. She was funny, efficient and took to my mother like they had been best friends all their lives. In fact my mother thought the woman was her best friend. We had a trial period and the whole thing worked so well, it was as if someone had taken the brake off and I could finally coast down the road. I began to breathe again. My load lightened, my mood lightened and my mother thought she had a best friend. Life was good in our little world. I decided that we'd make a regular date with my mother's best friend, as we called her. I'd work in my study and she'd just do what she did with my mother.

I could hear them chatting away in the kitchen one Friday and it struck me that my mother was much more garrulous with her friend than with me. I crept out to listen and was struck by the lucidity of the conversation.

'Oh, she's very busy,' my mother was saying. I thought it was said with a modicum of pride, until she added, 'not much time for me, but I can take care of myself.' She said it with rancour. No-one expects accolades when they do things, but to be put down so dismissively was a shock. I knew this wasn't my mother talking. I realised she wasn't in charge of what came out of her mouth, but it hurt just the same. All the things I'd done, all the sacrifices I made and she dismissed my efforts with a word on her sharp tongue. It's not my mother talking. I said it to myself over and over, in the hope I'd believe it.

My father's next anniversary came around and I missed it. My mother never knew and I didn't tell. Censoring her life felt wrong, but the end justifies the means. Why put her through the anguish, the sorrow all over again.

I pulled out the albums and we had an evening of going over the photographs instead.

'Remember you like champagne.'

'Yes.'

'Let's have a bottle.'

I slipped into taking control of her life so easily. She fell back on the tried and tested modus operandi of acquiescing. We all knew where we stood. It had taken a few trials and errors to get the balance. Now with our roles firmly set, we could coast. Once a week we would go somewhere, and life happened in between.

My mother answered my mobile phone while I was in the toilet and said yes. She could have been acceding to filling in for the Prime Minister on the weekend for all she knew of the conversation.

I rang back and it transpired she was invited to go on a motorbike ride on a Harley Davidson. They were having a charity ride and wanted my mother as a drawcard.

The word exploitation came to mind. How do people in the public eye deal with this sort of grasping? It was no use explaining to the fellow that my mother was incapable of making such a decision. She had said yes under the flimsiest of whims. He said she sounded keen. He said he was recording the conversation, for insurance purposes.

'I guess you've been on a motorbike?'

'Oh, yes. Hundreds of times.'

It was for a Children's hospital. A good cause, but aren't they all. We were picked up at our house and my mother was given a black leather jacket and helmet. She looked the part, but I could see that the glitch wasn't in residence. She looked terrified.

'Who are they?' she whispered to me.

It was a question that had a lot of back story. I didn't know how to explain that she had agreed for the charity, that she could be, and could do, anything. It was one of those days when she was befuddled.

'Look, I don't think my mother is up for this. She's had a rough couple of days.' It sounded a reasonable excuse. But they had garnered television coverage on the strength of my mother's appearance. They had expectations. Their expectations were beyond my mother's capacity.

'She'll be fine.' He said it so assuredly.

I dithered and watched my mother. She stood like someone who is about to get hit.

'No. I don't think she will be fine.'

'Look. All she needs to do is sit on the back of this bike. It's not rocket science.'

I glanced over at her nodding to the other riders, putting on a brave face.

And they deposited her on the bike. She gripped the man's jacket like her life depended upon it.

It was after they left that the word revenge popped up, to flap about in my conscience. I was truly evil.

She came back and went into a funk for a week. I didn't try to revive her. I worked around her and waited for her to rise like the phoenix. She didn't look happy and wasn't that why we were all trying so hard? I threw myself into work and waited. She moped and then slipped into the persona she knew so well. It was a perfect fit. The woman who was a passenger in life. I didn't ask anything of her and she didn't offer anything in return. We were suited to these roles, we'd been playing them all our lives.

But life is never set.

We were visited by a very persuasive power couple with a grand plan.

I listened and looked at my mother. She was the model of propriety. Butter wouldn't melt in her mouth.

'We'll let you think on it.' And they left,

their au de cologne wafting through the house to leave a bad smell.

My mother waved them off and then forgot about them. I couldn't forget.

They wanted my superstar to be airlifted onto the disabled persons yacht as it sailed up the Derwent in Tasmania on the last leg of the Sydney to Hobart New Year Yacht race.

It would be a boost, a coup for the Disability organisation and we were assured every safety measure would be employed. There would be insurance cover included.

How did we get here? How did we go from an organza dress to a helicopter ride and a prime spot on the yacht race? I must have been asleep at the wheel.

The offer needed to be finalised in a week. There would be promotional activities to organise. My mother was sleeping on the settee while I wrestled with the decision. There was no use asking her opinion or advice. She might say yes one moment and no the next. I had power of attorney, but this was something completely different. It would be madness. It was hairbrained. They were using my mother shamefully. But, it was for disability. They had every eventuality covered they said. It might just break down the stigma and sweep away the barriers of ignorance.

People might think a little differently about the older generation. I tossed up the for and against.

What if she was terrified? How could I be sure I was doing it all for the right reasons? We had a week to decide.

I didn't talk about it. My mother was happy in her world and on her clear days she slipped into the old persona so easily I didn't feel I could broach the subject. This would need to be my decision.

They came around to the house and sat down at my kitchen table. They had forms to fill in, things to sign, papers to read and mock-ups of the event. They were slick.

'We will take care of everything,' they said. Would they take care of my mother?

She had to go through some preliminary training. I wasn't sure they knew that she had little or no short term memory. You could have shown her how to press the red nuclear button and a minute later she ask, 'what's this?' They were covering their bases they said.

She would be strapped to a buddy all the time they told me. She became a thing.

There was to be a press conference before the beginning of the race and they wanted my mother front and centre. I don't think they realised how a stressful situation affects a person with dementia. Just asking them a question can send them into a fog. Words will not come their brain shuts off the boxes they need the most.

'No.' I said. They scrambled for an alternative. Could I say something on my mother's behalf? They had a script prepared. I needed to hit all the salient points, the charities that were involved, the thrill, the excitement of the event. My mother was strapped into a harness for a photo opportunity. I wanted to add that my mother and I were personally hoping this stunt would go some way to dispelling the myths about people with a disability. They cut me off for a weather report.

The race was a thrilling event for the leader boats. All the other craft had days ahead of them to get to Hobart. We were treated to a hotel in the vicinity of the Derwent River to wait for the arrival of the boat manned by people with disabilities.

As we watched the race unfold on the television set in our hotel room I became more nervous. What was I thinking? This was madness. My mother, in her blissful ignorance watched the race with little interest.

'Do you remember the boat trip to the reef?'

'Oh yes.' She had no idea.

We were summoned at the appropriate hour and taken to the airport. They took special care of my mother and went over the procedure noting that it was just like skydiving only she would be landing on a boat. She nodded and looked at me for confirmation. I gave her the thumbs up and hid behind my camera lens.

'She's one hellava woman your mother.' The man with the air traffic paddles winked at me.

What did he know? It made me angry that people assumed so much. They took my mother and morphed her into a commodity. A convenient thing.

She looked so small strapped onto the man in the orange jump suit. I could have run out before the rotors started. My voice failed me.

There was a whirring and then she was gone. I had failed my mother.

The power couple were all over me. They ushered me into a waiting limo and we were taken to a large marquee with an even larger screen. There were sponsors draped over the chairs, half tanked on cheap champagne, women serving who looked about twelve years old and half eaten food on the floor.

'Drink?'

'No thank you.' I watched the screen for the unfolding drama.

'This is gonna be great.' The man with all the answers punched my arm.

'Don't touch me,' I snapped. I had a large dose of self-loathing, I didn't need a feelgood snake oil merchant punching me on the arm.

They watched as everything unfolded like they said it would. I watched for the whites of her eyes. She was scared.

And then my miracle happened. She licked her lips, smiled and gave the thumbs up. The adrenalin rush was enough to push her over the edge and I could tell she passed out, others might have interpreted the head down as checking harnesses. The camera turned to the waiting boat. I went to find a toilet to throw up.

We waited on the dock for the boat to arrive to much cheering and flag waving. The power couple were congratulating themselves on a stunt that hit all the right markers. They were ready for their bonus. I looked for my mother amid the people and while I hunted I vowed never to be shystered into something like this ever again.

She waved from the cockpit and gave me the thumbs up.

'She was sea sick,' I heard a man say to his companion.

She was helped off the boat and pushed around for pictures. People draped themselves over her for the vicarious fame. She was in the spotlight, manipulated and manhandled. I stepped in and pushed a large man away from her.

'Get your grubby hands off my mother.' It came out with more force than I thought I had. He took a step back and then sneered at me.

'Cow.'

'Pig,' I said back.

A security guard stepped into the fray and pulled me away. I shrugged off his grip and tried to explain that the man was accosting my mother, but he was having none of my excuses.

'I think you've had quite enough drink.' It was a condescending attitude that got me fired up.

'I'll let you know when I've had enough,' I said.

'Come on missy.' The guard took my arm and began to lead me to the exit.

'My mother,' I pointed.

'Alright, Alright.' He pulled me back to my mother who was standing still in the melee. 'Come on.' We were escorted out.

I hailed a taxi back to our hotel and once there I put my mother to bed, fully clothed. She had had enough. I had had enough.

I sat on the edge of her bed and talked as she fell into a deep sleep. I tried to let her know that I was wrong. I told her I was sucker punched. I made her a promise it would never happen again. She wasn't a thing, a commodity, she was my mother.

And once home I eschewed every overture.

I became obsessive of our privacy, our routine. I didn't want anything to upset our world.

If needed we would become an island.

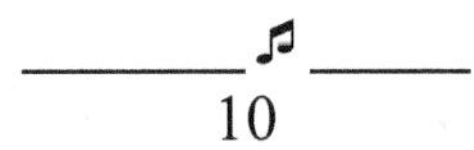

10

I made a pact with myself.

There would be no more derring-do.
There would be no more merry-go-round.
I withdrew us from the hurley-burley.

We took a week at a resort in the hills to collect ourselves and I would try to be a better person.

'Is it my birthday?'

'I believe it is.'

I could try to just let my mother live out her days or I could learn to like the woman. I decided the latter for the sake of my sanity. And so we started again.

Before she had come to live with me, I was a regular audience member of opera, concerts, art galleries. I couldn't imagine my mother enjoying any of this. My parents weren't highbrow or low brow. They didn't go in for much stimulation. My mother read, but her reading was confined to the romance of boy meets girl, boy loses girl, boy and girl get married. I wasn't such a snob to think that those books were any less entertaining than *War and Peace*, but there was a whole world out there that my mother could explore ... with me as her guide.

So we began to explore.

I bought a season ticket for her at the concert hall. There was a Brahms concert coming up and they were shipping in the organ from Bavaria. As season ticket holders we were in the privileged position of receiving extras. The extra would be a tour of the organ, a lecture on the history and canapes for after. I've always enjoyed an evening like this. You meet interesting people, mingle with the like-minded, and the catering is always top notch. Plus, you get to dress up.

We went shopping for outfits. My father had left a sizable bank balance for my mother and as the power of attorney, I knew she could splash out. She has always had a trim figure. She was one of those women who could wear a sack and it would look good. Naturally there was a temptation to dress her and have my tastes dripping off her shoulders, but I held back. I introduced her to fashion and we had a girl afternoon, trying on outfits, lunch and finished with a taxi ride home stuffed with goodies.

As an architect, my father often had dinners for work. My mother usually cried off these events, but on the odd occasion she attended, she looked stunning. Now as we dressed I saw myself as a young girl, buttoning up her dress at the back, watching her put on lipstick and when I woke up the next morning she'd be the mother I always wanted.

We entered the concert hall, conquering heroines. My mother was recognised, but the hoi-polloi were a different breed. They didn't gush. They didn't pry. It was noted and they moved on ... in different circles. I saw a few friends and we chatted, my mother at my side. It was a proud moment.

The evening was a success. She was happy. I was happy. We mingled after and drank champagne.

'Is it my birthday?'

'I think it is.'

Her interest in the recital was minimal. She just didn't connect and I could see she was having a hard time just processing where she was and why. Would it always be like this? What did it matter that she couldn't recall the recital a week after the event. I had taken photos and we looked at them like someone would look at a magazine in the doctors waiting room. They were interesting, but didn't elicit any recall. I didn't need to put my expectations on her.

There was a movie that I had an interest in seeing, because my old tutor was the photographic director. My mother didn't go to the cinema when I was growing up. She said she couldn't see the point of sitting in the dark, when a book would do, and that was the excuse I always heard. In fact, as I looked back, there was always a glib answer to an enquiry. Always the same answer as if she had a set that were given to her and they sufficed for every eventuality.

'I love the cinema.' She said it with a smile.

We frocked up for the premier, my tutor giving us two tickets, and had a ball. My mother laughed at the jokes and cried at the end. I'd never seen her exhibit her emotional side with such candour. We were treated to a supper with my tutor, and she fell asleep on his settee. It was all so easy, it lulled me before the storm. And the storm did come.

It gathered pace one afternoon when I was dealing with a work issue. I needed to concentrate, read contracts, email people and be fully absorbed. I still had a career, albeit an on/off freelance one since she came to stay.

She flumped down on the settee with exaggerated gestures. I tried to ignore it. She huffed. I slid my study door closed.

'Why do you hate me?'

I opened the door.

'Yes, you. Why do you hate me?' She said it with a spite that flicked a switch and I was in my childhood again. I'd said those words to her, as I perceived that my sister got all the attention.

'I don't hate you,' I said.

'You do. I'm not crazy you know.'

'I know that.'

As she launched into the most vicious tempest of words it brought me to tears. Here was the moment when all her boxes were opened. Every perceived slight, threat, feeling, emotion was on display. Her vitriol cut into my memories, stabbed at my past and infected my well built up story of my life. She accused me of every sin, she dashed my goodwill on barren ground and rubbed salt into my bleeding wounds. My childless status was thrown in my face. My selfishness at not providing grandchildren a stain she could never remove.

I knew that this wasn't my mother. I knew it, but I hit back.

Words can wound. I shouted at her, pointed my finger at her and told her the truth about who she was. My argument kept coming back to ungrateful and the things people did for her, her whole life. I jabbed her with a useless life, a loveless life, a life devoid of the finer feelings.

'You were a mistake.' The barb hit me on that tattoo the doctor had written on my heart.

How can you reconcile your life, when you hear that you were not wanted. Was this the truth? Was this her last hurrah?

She slept, and I drank. Once the words were out of the box they could never be put back. Never.

As far as my mother was concerned, the storm hadn't happened. I looked for remorse, for some sort of human emotion that I knew I wouldn't find. There would be no scars on her. She was bulletproof, cossetted in her own bubble. I so wished for a different mother. I wanted the other mother, I needed her.

I scoured the internet for some fictional books on human relationships. I'd get her to read about the tsunami of a cruel jab at the truth. She might ponder on the similarities. She dropped reading as if she never had an interest.

'You love reading,' I said.

'I hate it.'

I tried rented movies. She loved the old 1940s black and white movies and would play them all day. We went through every screwball comedy, every tear jerker and western. This was what people did with their kids. They plonked them down in front of the television. It was babysitting at its worst. But, it saved me. I could guarantee myself 90 minutes to work. I threw myself into working at home. It was better than trying too hard, which was exhausting and counter-productive, because it fed my loathing. Maybe I was a nasty person.

My group had never quite got over our flirt with the media and I felt a slow shunning. I thought these people were my compatriots in the line of fire. I thought we had something in common. They were only human after all.

'Let's go for a walk.'

I watched as she processed the request. There was a frown and a growing fog around her brow.

We strolled around the block and it was the first time she'd seen the gardens, the houses and listened to the history.

'He died right in that house.' I knew some of the story about the gangster house. We stood and looked at the upstairs windows.

'I always wanted an upstairs.' She said it and I almost believed that the woman I knew as my mother was back. 'But your father said we had a rock solid foundation right where we were.' My mother smiled at me. 'He was right.'

Did she realise the allegory in my father's words?

'Did you love him?' The question had been on my lips for most of my life.

'Oh yes. Hundreds of times.' A glib answer in times of stress.

As the days progressed the fog came down just about every day. She could watch a movie and then in half an hour watch it again for the first time. She slept more. She ate less.

I had the chance to do a photo shoot overseas. It would be three weeks of work and good money. Three weeks might be a lifetime for me and just a moment for my mother. I could put her in the hill retreat, they'd pamper her, plonk her in front of the television, and do her nails. Or, I could take her on a trip one last time. She was physically able, but would she be in too much of a fog.

The doctor said if I thought I could cope, then why not.

It was useless to prep my mother, we would just wing it, moment by moment.

_______ ♫ _______
11

Living in the moment can be exhilarating and at the same time exhausting. For my mother it was just another day, and because she didn't have the day before for reference it wasn't a problem.

Our journey would take us to a place I never thought we'd go together.

I fitted my mother with an alarm, slung around her neck she look official, rather than needy. She had a phone in her bag, primed with my number and her GPS always on. Throughout her time with me she'd never forgotten her handbag. It was like an extension of her whole life.

I had every eventuality covered and we boarded the plane with a bigger checklist than the pilot. She was placid, sleepy and content. She woke up for food, but with movies to watch she settled easily.

Our hotel was in the centre of town and in the taxi, under stress, I could see her face change to the mother I always wanted. She sat a little straighter and smiled at me.

'I remember that,' she pointed to a landmark.

'Yes. I'm sure you do.'

Our room was at the back of the hotel overlooking a courtyard with a small shrub garden and a couple of chairs for smokers. We sat on our balcony and watched the sun go down, drinking a G & T from the minibar.

'Are you ok?'

'Oh yes,' she said. I hoped it was true.

As she slept in the single bed next to mine, I wondered if she dreamed. Did she have wild adventures or was hers the slumber of the dead. I couldn't help but notice her boxes in the matrix were being closed off, archived quicker than I imagined.

My work was at a studio and I'd prepped then to expect my mother in tow. They were really good about it and had allocated a young woman to chaperone my mother while I worked.

'She likes coffee and cake,' I said as they left.

'It's my birthday you know,' I heard my mother say.

Our evenings were our own and I

contacted an associate to procure two tickets to a Rachmaninov concert. I've always like Rachmaninov and Concerto number 2 my favourite. My mother had never indulged in music, but I felt it was a vital tool to being human. It could transport you to places you never imagined. It could bring out what it was to feel, think and just be a sentinel being. It was magic.

It was in my third grade that something happened to me in regard to music. We had music once a week, broadcast from a speaker on the wall. This day, a warm afternoon when the insects buzzed and the weatherboard schoolroom ticked as it heated we were allowed to put our heads on the desk and just listen. What issued forth was the Peer Gynt Suite. I'd never in my life heard anything so wonderful. I began to cry at the beauty I could hear. Why hadn't someone told me something like this existed. Why didn't I know. It was music that took me to another place, a place that no-one else might enter. That feeling has stayed with me ever since that day. As I grew up I bought records, then cassettes, then CDs and finally a digital library of music.

We went shopping and frocked up for the event. The concert hall was nothing like the one at home. This had the chandeliers, the marble staircase, the opulence, the sense of occasion. Our seats were on the aisle as I had requested. If it all went to hell, we could make an exit without too much fuss.

She was nervous, but there was a spark of surprise in her eye. I was nervous and longed for my other mother to emerge just as the lights dimmed.

Then, as the music began to fill the auditorium, to build and swirl around us, my mother took my hand ... and squeezed. The physical contact was like an electric shock. I had almost forgotten she was there as the music worked it's magic. Did she feel what I felt? Was this what had been missing in her life. Was the answer as simple as music?

I watched her utter rapture. This really was the first time in her life she felt the magic.

I had mixed feelings and hated my father for never letting my mother spread her wings. How could he have shackled her so utterly that her spark of life was snuffed. He was the monster to deny her music, laughter and light. He was to blame for her dependency. It was like the Stockholm syndrome. She was in love with her captor and could never escape. I convinced myself she was a victim. I had found the key and could save her.

I felt like an explorer and threw myself

into my discovery. We got tickets to other concerts and I waited for the music to work it's magic. She loved it. She loved everything about classical music. She'd sit and close her eyes and be transported to another place. I loved the thought that she could feel what I felt. We weren't so different after all.

'I love this,' she whispered as we settled into our seats for a recital of the Four Seasons by Vivaldi. She smiled at me. 'Thank you,' she mouthed and she kissed me on the cheek. I held my breath and hoped it wasn't a glitch in the matrix. It was a gold moment.

My work complete we spent the day shopping.

I bought her some earbuds, and a library of music. I set it all up on her phone and she only had one button to press. She had classical, jazz, and everything in between.

She didn't have an idea where she was, and her brow furrowed as she looked for something familiar.

'Where are we?'

I ushered her into a café and sat her down. Perhaps I was pushing her too much? She seemed to have the physical stamina, but her brain was being sorely tested.

'We are in a café, having fun,' I said. The fog descended until she spied the opulent display of cakes.

'I cooked once you know.'

'Yes, I know.'

We indulged in a high afternoon tea and gushed over our shopping haul. She was in a good mood, a lovely mood to end our trip. I watched her lick the cream from her cake, a dab dangled on her nose. I took her napkin and wiped it off.

She laughed. It was such a delightful sound. My mother laughed. My real mother laughed and it was the most wonderful sound in the world.

'Your father often took me out, you know.'

'Yes.'

'We had such fun.'

Her memory was genuine as the fog lifted and a box opened for a moment. I wanted to tell her he was a monster. How had he kept this woman so bereft of life.

She looked at her wedding ring and twisted it around her finger. The inscription had long worn away, but her finger found it none-the-less.

'For ever and always.' She said it with tenderness. She loved my father for all his faults. Who was I to pontificate on their married life. I only saw eighteen years of it.

'He was a good man.' Her lucid moment pricked at my assumptions.

'Mum?'

'A good man.' She said and I leaned over to hold her hand.

Our trip over, the photographs put in her pictorial diary, we settled back into walking, taking one moment at a time. Instead of movies she listened to music. I would suggest a playlist and she'd sit back to be captivated.

We established a routine where at the end of the day we'd sit and listen to something together. I may crack a bottle of champagne; a few snacks and we'd let the music wash over us. It was a calming end to the day. I looked forward to it, and in some respects it satisfied my initial fantasy of sunsets, companionship and quiet contemplation.

I didn't wonder if this was my mother or an incarnation, what mattered was the moment and she taught me that. My mother lived in the moment, she didn't have a choice. Her moments were like a string of pearls making up a life. Each moment was perfect on its own.

Her scrap book was getting bigger as our adventures built so I decided to put them in a book. Whether she would recognise herself in the book I didn't know, but it was what I wanted to do, probably more for myself than her.

I could make lasting memories in photographs, the beauty of capturing a moment was the essence of why I loved the medium. Life could swirl around you and yet with the opening of the lens you could capture something forever. It distilled life to a moment, the irony of the words not lost on my situation.

When the book arrived fully formed we had a party. I invited a few friends, we made it an occasion to remember, although she wouldn't remember. The book gave her great delight. She looked at the pictures and marvelled at the woman on the pages. The dresses, the concerts, the ticket stubs, it was all there. She looked at the skydiving woman in the pictures and shook her head in disbelief. It didn't matter that she couldn't remember the joy, the terror, the thrill. Her moments were precious at the time.

It wasn't her whole life, but perhaps it was the life she might have lived.

We drank too much, ate too much and celebrated my mother's life while there was still a little of her in this world. I watched her from across the room as she sat with my friend and they pointed out the woman in the pictures. She was enjoying the fun of the moment. She caught me looking and for one second I saw my mother. She smiled.

'Is it my birthday?'

'I'm sure it is.'

_______ ♫ _______

A strange kind of paradise,
Is the moment of release.
Of battles won
decisions made
and a conscience at peace.

H.E. Ashwin

www.ingramcontent.com/pod-product-compliance
Lightning Source LLC
LaVergne TN
LVHW050614200726

843508LV00010B/1856